Three Times Lucky

Other Works by Byron Gordon

<u>Novellas</u>
The Girl In Brown
Arminium
Spectre Of War

<u>Short Stories</u>
Mistress Or Mate
Business Or Pleasure
A Lion In The Snow
George And The Dragon
Giant Slayer
Log Of The El Dorado
Spook's Hill
Diamond Of The Serengeti
More Than A Flesh Wound
The Bhut Jolokia Caper
Stark Salvation
A Petty Slight
Gentleman's Debt

Three Times Lucky

The Chronicles of the Holy Isles

Byron Gordon

Copyright © 2013 Byron Gordon

"The Angel's Halo" copyright © Byron Gordon, 2012.
First published on www.marieabmare.wordpress.com.
Reprinted by permission of the author.

"The Vampiric Archipelago" copyright © Byron Gordon, 2012.
First published on www.marieabmare.wordpress.com.
Reprinted by permission of the author.

"The Fertile Plain" copyright © Byron Gordon, 2012.
First published on www.marieabmare.wordpress.com.
Reprinted by permission of the author.

All rights reserved.

First Edition
ISBN: 978-1482005653

Set in Garamond
Printed in the United States of America

A Marie Ab Mare Publishing Book
www.marieabmare.wordpress.com

CONTENTS

Foreword	-
The Angel's Halo	1
The Vampiric Archipelago	17
The Fertile Plain	35

FOREWORD

These stories are adapted from the pen and paper RPG's I enjoyed with my brother and sister. My siblings endowed Sir James Flickerflame and Wain the Barbarian with far more complex and in-depth characterization than I would have managed on my own and taught me how to relax and tell a fun story. I feel no shame in admitting that these stories are not driven by plot. Instead the plots, such as they are, exist as a framework for the two friends to interact with each other and give everyone a good laugh. In my utterly un-biased opinion, this is cheesy sword and sorcery at its best.

I hope you enjoy their adventures as much as we did. Thank you.

The Angel's Halo

Sir James Flickerflame waffled outside the bishop's palace. He took a deep breath and straightened his tunic, double checking for stains on the pure white fabric. Then he adjusted the white cloak on his shoulders and shifted his sword belt a tiny bit. He took another deep breath and pounded on the gate. He muttered to himself, "Remember James, stay cool, stay confident. You are a paladin, stay cool."

He was so focused on staying cool and maintaining an indifferent air that when the warden flung open the gate James almost jumped out of his boots. He could feel a faint blush crossing his cheeks as he was ushered in.

"Sir Flickerflame," he announced his name to the warden.

ॐ Byron Gordon

"Ah, Sir Flickerflame," the warden said. "My lord, his Holiness, Dref Cefel, the kind, the pure, the devout," the warden shot a sideways glance at James, "the blessed, is waiting for you. I will lead you to him now."

"Lead the way then." James wanted to get the audience over with as soon as possible. He did not like talking to his superiors, it made him nervous. He swallowed, trying to banish his fears.

The warden wasted no time in leading him to the door to Bishop Cefel's audience chamber. Then the door was open and James strode in, looking confident, looking cool, and feeling like he was about to fall apart.

"I greet you in peace and the grace of God," said the bishop.

"I come in peace and the g-g-grace of G-G-God," stuttered James. He could feel his cheeks flaming red and the sangfroid with which he had walked into the room deserted him, laughing softly in his ear as it left.

"I have a quest for you." Dref Cefel affected not to notice the stutter. "I know that you only just left sanctuary and are young and inexperienced, untried and untested…"

James wished that the bishop would stop. He felt more and more insignificant with every word Cefel uttered.

"…But your dedication and devoutness has attracted attention and all our experienced paladins are on the mainland, fighting back the tide of evil blackness, that threatens our very church and the children of God, so we had to pick you to go on this quest."

"I am honored," said James hollowly. He would rather continue to lead Vespers at the corner chapel where he went every evening. "What exactly am I supposed to quest for?"

"The Angel's Halo is a crown that makes the wearer seem to be the most beautiful, the most charming, the most trustworthy woman in the world."

"I will be sure not to put it on." James lips moved before he could stop them.

The older man seemed not to notice. "It was given to an already beautiful woman, Gertrude the Lovely, but she went on a little cruise this spring and never returned. She set sail on the Lucitano, which was a ship blessed, not only by her presence, but one that sailed in the light. The sails were made of the purest white, finest gossamer silk and…"

"Excuse me," James interrupted, though horrified that he had just cut off one of the most powerful men on the Isle. "Where was this vessel last seen headed?"

"Towards that haven of all that is good and green. That place where true beauty is seen from the time the sun rises to the time it sets, that place where she desired to go more than any other. That place that has remained untainted by the evil which plagues the mainland. That place that contains only plant life native to it. That place…"

Encouraged by the success of his last interruption James did it again. "What is the place called, Your Holiness?"

"The Peaceful Isle. It is not far from our own Holy Island on whose blessed soil, as you probably know, we are now standing."

"How shall I get there?"

"You and your companion shall sail there. A boat has been made ready for you at the docks."

"My c-c-companion," James stuttered, caught off guard.

"Yes, we are sending a bodyguard with you, some barbarian from the north." Dref Cefel gestured to one of the deeper shadows off to the side. From the shadow moved a small mountain of a man, with a large sword strapped over his back. His hair hung to his shoulders and he wore nothing more than a pair of leggings and his battle harness. He grinned oafishly at James and gave a little shy wave, until he noticed the paladin's stare.

"What are you looking at?" he growled. "Do I have two butts or something?"

"No," replied James truthfully. After all he was a paladin, everything he did was truthful. "You are awfully short, I always thought barbarians were taller."

"I may be short but," the barbarian paused for a minute, "but you wear sissy clothes." He grinned again, like he had just won some kind of contest. James turned back to Bishop Cefel.

"Do I have to take him?" he asked plaintively.

Three Times Lucky ∞

"Yes," sighed the bishop. "But don't worry if he dies, he's just a barbarian, after all."

"My name is Wain," growled the barbarian. "And I don't die."

"Very well Your Holiness. With your leave I will go and complete this quest as quickly as I can." James bowed and backed out of the hall. Wain followed, walking with his back to the bishop. Once they were out of the audience chamber James glared at him.

"Do not ever turn your back on the Bishop! Never, do you understand, you rude idiot?" lectured James severely.

"Wotcher," replied Wain. "But I think you're the rude one. Calling me names and you never introduced yourself."

As they continued out of the palace James drew himself up importantly. "My name is," he paused for effect, "Sir James Flickerflame. You may call me Master Flickerflame."

"Wotcher James." Wain's head snapped around. "There's a bar. Can we stop?"

"W-W-What?" James was caught off guard, but still mentally chastised himself for stuttering in front of his new associate, "No. We must hurry to the docks and get our boat."

"All right," Wain said. "But I'm thirsty."

James was struck by a brilliant idea. "Why don't you go get a drink, actually. I will make sure the boat is ready."

Wain started for the bar like a hound dog after a hambone, but then turned. "You don't get rid of me that easily. I am coming on this quest and getting my fair share of glory and booze."

James sighed. "Very well."

They continued down to the docks in silence, until they reached the man that handled the bishop's boating ventures.

As James explained what they needed the man groomed the long goatee sprouting from his chin. It looked like he had a tail growing out from under his lip and hanging to his belt buckle. The long strands of hair were all gray despite the man's full head of dark hair..

"The Bish set aside this new boat we just got. She's a beaut," he said, pointed out a weathered looking little sloop.

"Only been owned once," the man continued, as they walked over to it, "by a little old lady who only took it out once a month. Barely thirty-five leagues on it and a better paint job…"

Wain turned and grabbed the man's lower lip tail, yanking hard. A great wad of hair came off in his hand and the man's face screwed up in the most unimaginable grimace of pain and horror. He started to jump up and down, screaming and clawing at his chin. Then he flung himself on the ground and rolled back and forth, screaming and kicking at the air.

"Why did you have to do that?" asked James with a sigh.

"I don't like used boat salesmen," replied Wain, as he undid the moorings.

Three Times Lucky ఴ

"Well, next time punch the guy or step on his toes," said James as he raised the sail. "But don't pull out his beard."

"The guy looked like a goat," snorted Wain, as he steered the boat away from the dock. "I was doing him a favor."

Behind them the man rolled off the dock into the water and his screaming was replaced by a muffled glub-a-glub sound. With the sail raised and a stiff breeze at their backs Sir James and Wain set off in the direction of the Peaceful Isle.

By the next morning they could see land on the horizon. Their voyage had been pleasant, with smooth seas and a good breeze, but, as they neared the island, storm clouds rolled in and lightning cracked across the sky. The thunder that followed was so loud it made them jump. The waves started to get larger and larger and Wain, in the bow of the boat, stuck his head over the side, looking green about the gills.

Rain lashed them and the howling wind drove the small boat towards the island. James could feel the timbers under his feet squeal and creak, the boat seemed to shiver with eagerness and dove into the high seas like a duck into a pond. From James' point of view things couldn't get worse, but they suddenly did.

"Bleaugh!" Said Wain. Then he cried. "Captain, rocks ahead! Bleaugh!"

"What?" Shouted James. "What is Bleaugh?"

"I'm throwing, bleaugh, up," Wain shouted back.

"Oh." James was silent for a minute. "Tell me where the rocks are so I can steer around them."

"There's one, bleaugh, dead ahead," shrieked back Wain.

James wrenched the steering oar to the starboard side, hard. The boat nearly capsized and Wain was flung against the bulkhead. Just as he stood up James returned to his previous course with the same sharpness. Wain was flung against the opposite bulkhead.

"Oof," Wain roared. "What was that for?"

"Stop whining and watch for rocks," shouted James.

"Ok, ok." Wain returned to watching. "To the left, the left, THE LEFT. THE OTHER LEFT. OH MY GOSH!"

The boat struck the rock with a glancing blow and rebounded into the sea with the sound of splintering wood. The entire frame of the boat quivered from bow to stern. Wain was once more flung against the bulkhead but this time he held on as he got back up.

"I told you that rock was there," Wain hollered, "and you steered right for it. Let me drive."

"You told me to go left," James shook his head.

"No!" Shouted Wain. "I told you the rock was going left and… HOLY SMOKES, GO RIGHT, GO RIGHT, GO STARBOARD FOR CRYING OUT LOUD! LOOK OUT ROCKS, THERE'S A CRAZY DRIVER!"

James wrenched the boat to the right and then left again to comply with Wain's frenzied shouting. The short, stocky barbarian reminded James of a wet monkey, jumping up and down on the bow of the boat, hooting and hollering. Finally they managed to sail in to a small pier that jutted out from the island. Wain, battered but cheerful to be setting foot on dry land, threw the mooring lines over a piling and pulled the boat up close to the pier. James stepped onto the pier and a wild looking man, with dark skin and rusty armor jumped out from behind a convenient nearby bush.

"You shall not pass." He spoke in a voice that was as deep as a chasm. Then he cackled, as if aware of how corny he sounded.

"I am a holy paladin of God," said James, trying, and failing, to make his voice as deep as the wildman's. "You shall not block my path."

He started to walk forward towards the man, trying to look cool and confident. The man drew his short sword and assumed a fighting stance. James paused, considering his options. He had been taught the way of the sword while in sanctuary but he had never thought that he would have to use the one he owned.

"Can we talk about this?"

"Never!" Shrieked the wild warrior. "I am a dark human, opposed to the church in any form. We must fight to the death!"

"Fine. But my sword is bigger than yours," taunted James as he drew his sword. "En garde!"

He was about to engage the dark human in mortal combat, prepared to give his last breath in a dramatically desperate struggle to complete his quest. His opponent rushed to join the battle, a crazy light flashing through his eyes. Then a bee hummed by James' ear and the dark human fell to the deck, rolled into the water, and slowly sank under the weight of his armor.

"Darnit," said Wain. "That was my favorite arrow!"

James' mouth dropped open. "You shot him!"

"Yeah." Wain nodded. "And lost my favorite arrow!"

"But what about honorable combat?"

"Oh, that is all well and good, but winning is important too."

"I would have won!" Said James.

"You were about to get your butt kicked," laughed Wain.

"Humph." Since James happened to secretly agree with that idea he couldn't argue. After all he was a paladin and always told the truth.

The island they had landed on was mostly a large meadow with a stream running through the middle of it. Peaceful breezes gently swayed the graciously green blades of grass. The southern side of the island was cloaked with oak trees, their branches waving peacefully in the breeze. Small, pretty birds twittered peacefully and fluttered back and forth through the trees as they pursued each other in a pleasant game of tag. A stone bridge gracefully crossed the stream that divided the island.

Three Times Lucky 〜

"Let's see if there is any clue at the bridge." James started walking in that direction.

"Ok." Wain glanced around nervously as they walked. "This place is too peaceful."

"I think its nice," replied James as they reached the bridge. There were some footprints in a small patch of mud at the foot of the bridge.

"Look at these." James knelt to examine them. "Can you track them?"

He looked up when the silence started to grow awkward. "You can track, can't you?"

"Well." Wain looked embarrassed. "I only made it to the Cubscout level, but I'll try to see... LOOK OUT!" He drew his sword and swung it wildly at James.

"You treacherous punk," cried James as he rolled to the side. "You'll pay for..."

He stopped short as he saw Wain was not attacking him but the ten foot troll that had snuck up on them. James changed his tune quickly. "Get him Wain! Ooh look out!. And now the left slash... and thrust!"

Wain drove the troll back under the bridge and disappeared after it. James sighed. The first rule of fighting trolls was that you never entered their dens until after they were dead. He heard Wain yell and swiftly peeked under the bridge. Neither Wain nor the troll were visible. James said a short prayer for his friend.

"No... I am not his friend, just his associate," muttered James angrily. He started towards the woods. He figured that if anyone else was on the island they would have to be there, because he could see everywhere else. He walked through the oaks and soon caught the smell of a campfire. Following it led him to where a man and a woman were cooking some form of food for the midday meal. The woman was the most stunningly beautiful lady he had ever seen and he instantly recognized her as Gertrude.

"Thank you," James told the man. "For keeping her safe. There is a monstrous troll on this island and it must have been a difficult task."

"Don't thank him." Gertrude glared at the man. "He must be returned to the Holy Isle to be burnt. We must save his soul. He is a runere!"

Sir James Flickerflame gasped in shock and horror.

Wain gasped, filling his lungs with air before the troll pulled him back underwater. After he pursued the monster under the bridge it disappeared. He had walked cautiously into the cave that was hollowed out, only to find that there was a submerged pit deep enough for the troll to hide in. The monster had grabbed him by the ankles and pulled him under. Only by biting the troll very hard had he managed to get away long enough to get that breath of fresh air. But it was enough.

Back underwater Wain came to grips with the monstrosity and began choking it with one hand around its throat, squeezing as only a barbarian can (which is extremely hard). He drew his hunting knife

Three Times Lucky ஐ

with his free hand and slashed and cut at the troll until it got one hand around his throat and choked him as only a troll can (which is a lot harder than a barbarian can). His vision going dark and his movements becoming sluggish Wain let loose the rage that constantly boiled within him and convinced the troll to become a professional sword swallower. (Now you may ask how the troll, without prior experience, could become a professional sword swallower so quickly. Unfortunately for the troll his career ended swiftly with his first attempt as a long piece of steel got stuck in his throat.) As he faded into the realm of unconsciousness Wain floated to the surface of the flooded pit. He took a long shuddering gasp of air. Then another. Then another and another and he regained consciousness. Shaking his head, he crawled and splashed into the trolls cavern where he found a small stash of money and the Angel's Halo.

Careful to not even accidentally put on the Halo, he counted the money and slipped it into his pouch.

"No need to tell James about the money. It's not like he drinks!" Wain reasoned with his keen barbarian intellect.

Then he splashed out from under the bridge and studied the tracks to find out where James had gone. Satisfied that he had got it right he set off for the trees, towards the source of all the screaming and yelling.

○3 Byron Gordon

Now where is that confounded barbarian, thought James as he leapt sideways through the air, barely dodging a fire bolt that the man had shot from a piece of wood. I do wish that girl would shut up, he thought, as Gertrude screamed again.

Apparently the runere thought the same because he turned to her and shouted, "Shut up!"

Then he whirled back and shot another fire bolt at James, who dodged in turn. He couldn't get close enough to the man to use his sword because of the constant barrage of fire bolts. There was smoke steadily rising from several parts of the underbrush but he didn't have time to see if they could be put out. He jumped again, dodging another bolt of flame.

He was so busy dodging that he kept on doing so, even though he saw the arrow that pierced through the man's heart. Even though he saw the wooden wand fall from lifeless fingertips. Then, suddenly embarrassed to be seen hopping and rolling about like a fool, he performed several karate kicks to the forest fires and put them out. He turned to see Gertrude gazing adoringly at Wain.

"My hero," she cried. "I was in grave danger and you braved the perilous battle to rescue me."

Wain just scuffed his feet and turned bright red as she gave him an enormous hug and a quick kiss on the cheek.

"But aren't you a little short for a barbarian?" She asked, pulling back. "And why are you so wet? How old are you?"

Three Times Lucky ෨

James watched Wain's embarrassed red face turn to an angry red face. He swooped in and pulled Gertrude away before the barbarian did something uncouth.

"You must forgive my companion," James said softly. "He was enchanted at birth by an evil runere to always be short and he is rather sensitive about it. Now, where is the Halo?"

"Oh," Cried Gertrude. "Woe is me for I have lost it!"

"What?"

"The evil troll stole it from me," she explained.

"Well I stole it back from him," growled Wain, tossing the gold circlet at her as he pushed past. "I'm going to the boat James. I'm leaving as soon as I can cast off lines!"

"He wouldn't leave us here," said Gertrude positively. Then a little hesitantly she asked, "Would he?"

"No!" replied James. "But we had better hurry, just to be safe."

He hurried her out to the boat. They arrived just in time to hop aboard as Wain steered the boat away from the pier.

It was a calm return journey to the Holy Isle and Sir James Flickerflame delivered Gertrude the Lovely safely to Bishop Dref Cefel. The bishop was pleased, except to see 'the barbarian' again. He commended James on how well he had completed the assignment, even with 'the barbarian' slowing him down and ordered him to await his next mission. Dismissed the

Byron Gordon

two heroes walked out of the palace gates and down the street. Wain's head snapped around.

"There's a bar. Can we stop?"

James checked a nearby sundial. "I have time for a beer before vespers," he smiled.

"Say," said Wain. "I must be rubbing off on you. I noticed that you lied to Gertrude about the curse of shortness, too. I thought paladins didn't lie."

"How do you know I was lying?" James grinned at Wain. "Do you remember what happened when you where born?

Wain shook his head thoughtfully. "No but how could you. You weren't there."

"Are you sure?" James paused for effect. "Perhaps I am your father!"

"What a load of troll dung!" Wain snorted.

The Vampiric Archipelago

"Pater et Filius et Spiritus Sanctus." Sir James recited slowly.

"Pater et filets sans tush," repeated Wain, trying to imitate the soothing chant.

"No." James shook his head. "Not quite."

"Well. I'm trying!"

You are making good progress..."

"One word every two hours!"

"Well..."

"I'll just move my lips, ok?"

"I guess that will be all right. Especially since it is time to go or we will be late." James sighed. "Don't tell me you're bringing your sword?"

"Why not?" Wain looked up from buckling his sword belt.

"One does not simply take a sword to Vespers!"

❧ Byron Gordon

"But..."

"Leave your sword here." James led Wain out of their tenement and onto the cobbled street.

"Ok, ok. I don't know why I let you talk me into this."

"You wanted to come," protested James, "I didn't talk you into anything!"

"I wanted to get the snacks afterward."

"You mean the social hour?" A young page slid to a stop in front of them. "Can we help you?"

"My lords, the Bishop Dref Cefel desires your presence immediately."

"We shall be there anon," said James and the page rushed off.

"Sounds like I should have brought my sword."

"He probably just wants to present us with an award or something."

"Huh, we'll see."

✦

Later, as they were ushered into the Bishop's chambers, James began to think that Wain might have been right. After all, surely the Bishop would give them advance notice of an award.

"I welcome you, Sir James Flickerflame, in the name of the Lord Almighty," said the Bishop. "I hope that my sudden summons has not inconvenienced you."

"Not at all, your Holiness," James assured him.

"Huh, I missed my first Vespers and Snack Hour," grumbled Wain.

Three Times Lucky ෨

"It has recently been brought to my attention," the Bishop affected not to notice Wain, "that a conclave of evil knights, know as Vampires, has taken over the old island stronghold of the Order of the Sea. In times now past this fortress served as the home for the monks and knights who made it their duty to save those in peril from the sea. It is a great shame to see such a proud and pure place desecrated by a brood of villainous pirates in this manner."

"Indeed a terrible shame," said James. "We must do something about this."

"Our current intelligence indicates that the Order of the Sea possessed the Shining Shield and the Sword of Truth. If at all possible it would be a great help to have these artifacts recovered. Their presence on the front would greatly inspire the troops, for they are currently hard pressed to hold what little ground we have gained."

"We will leave as soon as possible, my lord," said James. "Do we have transportation?"

"A vessel will be provided. You will speak to our agent at the docks. It will be a different man this time. Shortly after you departed to the Peaceful Isle our agent was nowhere to be found. Most peculiar." Again the Bishop pretended not to notice Wain's guffaws.

"Very well. If you'll excuse me, my lord." James bowed and backed out of the hall, with Wain in his wake.

◎   Byron Gordon

As soon as they were out of the hall James turned angrily to Wain, "Try to maintain a little more decorum when we are before the Bishop."

"I was good," protested Wain. "I wanted to treat the ol' Bish to my chant."

"Well, at least you didn't do that. Now speak his name with respect."

"Ok, ok." Wain sighed. "You're no fun, man."

"Let's go and prepare our gear. We are leaving early in the morning."

The next morning they were happy to see that the new dock agent did not have a goatee. He was an old, tough looking sailor with an anchor tattooed on one of his brawny forearms. A lit pipe jutted from his mouth, holding up an enormous mustache.

"Good morn to ye, sirs. The Bishop said that you'd be ah coming for one oh me vessels. All I have kin be crewed by two lubbers be the Maid of Light. She be a right merry Maid, aye, she'll do fine by you ifen you do fine by her, know what I mean?"

"Excellent, thank you," said James.

"I hate boats," said Wain.

"Ah, now me lad. Don be asaying that. Frightful bad luck it tis, aye, turrible bad luck. The Bishop said I was to give you this here chart and compass. Aye, so's you kin find your way to the island."

"Thank you," said James again. "Cast off, Wain."

"Good luck to ye, sirs," called the old seaman.

Three Times Lucky ෨

They sailed the Maid of Light out onto the open ocean and brought their bearing around to the island. The entire day they made remarkable speed, the Maid of Light seemed to glide over the waves instead of sailing through them, but as night fell the vessel slowed.

"Hey!" yelled Wain.

"What?"

"I'm getting wet!"

"It's the spray," James said.

"No, I mean my feet are getting soaked. I think the boat is leaking."

"Don't be silly." James paused suddenly as water lapped at his feet. "Wain! Start bailing!"

"I hate boats," Wain grumbled as he bailed with his helmet.

The sun rose the next morning to gaze down upon two weary warriors, barely able to lift their arms to empty their bails. As the sun beams struck the waves the boat's seams mysteriously closed and the vessel picked up speed, once again floating on top of the waves. Switching off and on at the tiller, James and Wain arrived at the island.

There were three islands. High cliffs jutted up from the ocean and the islands perched on top, safe from the crashing waves. Dangerous looking shoals carpeted the sea between the islands and the ocean boiled and foamed like a witch's cauldron.

James sailed the Maiden of Light around the islands, skirting the shoals, looking for a good beach to land upon. It was a long and futile search. There was no point at which the islands sloped down to the sea, and as the afternoon faded Wain began to grumble about spending another night in the boat. Although James privately agreed he kept a stiff upper lip and said nothing. After all, appearances must be maintained.

Finally they spotted a rope dangling from one of the cliffs, hanging down to the surface of the water. After a heated debate James decided to risk the shoals and sail in to the rope. The paladin carefully maneuvered the boat into the breaking surf, while Wain stood in the bow calling out directions.

It took all of James' skill to keep the boat safe but finally they reached the rope. Wain grabbed it and gave a solid tug to ensure that it would hold his weight. The sea heaved them dangerously close to the cliff but a skillful turn of the tiller moved them from harms way. Then James moved up to the bow and began to climb as Wain held the rope. James had made it about halfway up when a powerful swell smashed the boat against the cliff. The timbers groaned in protest, and splintered, opening an enormous hole in the side.

"James!" screamed Wain. "James!"

"What?" James made the mistake of looking down and his hands froze onto the rope.

"I can't swim, James!"

"Climb, Wain! Climb!" James started to climb faster.

Though the rope creaked ominously, it held and they both made it to the top. Looking back down they

Three Times Lucky ಐ

watched as the Maiden of Light was shattered against the cliff side and sank beneath the foaming seas. Then they both looked at each other.

"The Bishop is not going to be happy," said James.

"I'm not worried about the Bishop," replied Wain, "I'm worried about ol' Popeye. We just sank his baby."

"No help for it now," James sighed. "Let us find this stronghold."

A forest grew to the very edge of the cliff, with trees leaning over the empty drop in a desperate struggle for sunlight. Despite the heavy undergrowth Wain lead them to where a small village sat in the center of the island. A tower stood guard over it all and they could make out a sentry standing watch at the top. As they looked out of the forest upon the village they heard the crunching of feet through the underbrush.

"Wait here," Wain whispered and disappeared.

James listened hard but couldn't hear anything but the tromping feet. Suddenly they stopped and a cry was cut short. James rushed through the bushes to where the sound had come from. He saw that Wain had ambushed a woodcutter and was holding him in a headlock. When the peasant saw James his face brightened.

"Let him go, Wain." Ordered James. "He is just an innocent woodcutter."

"You have come to save us?"

"We have come to exterminate the evil knights that have taken over the island. What can you tell us of them?"

"I don't know much, except that they are frightful to even be around. You can always tell when they are near because everything goes quiet and you suddenly get scared for no reason."

"How many men are in that tower?" Asked Wain.

"I don't know, but the Order of the Sea probably does."

"I thought they were all dead," said James.

"Well, some of our lads reformed them to fight the Vampires. Haven't had much luck yet. But I can get them to contact you out here."

"All right, have them come out here tonight. We'll be around."

"James, I don't like this," said Wain as the woodcutter walked away. "What if that man is a spy and he betrays us?"

"Then we will only have to fight about half of the soldiers in the tower out here and then the other half in the tower."

"What if they surprise us?"

"We will keep a good watch. Besides, we are sure to hear these guys coming. They cannot be very good woodsmen."

They made camp and settled in to await the Order of the Sea. Wain was standing first watch, sitting in front of their campfire, feeding twigs into it one at a time, when he felt a peculiar feeling of dread creeping over him. He shook James awake.

"Hmmf, is it time already?" James mumbled.

"Something is out there. I can feel it."

"Nonsense, it is your..." James trailed off.

Three Times Lucky

"You can feel it too!"

"It is like the woodcutter described. Frightful to..." a hollow laugh interrupted James and he screamed and took off like a scalded hare, fleeing through the woods. Wain was not far behind. As they dodged around a large tree they split up. James could feel that something was following him and desperately tried to regain his wits. Suddenly he felt shame pouring through him. He was a paladin and here he was, behaving like a child. A paladin stood up and fought evil, he did not flee from it.

Mustering his courage James stopped short (the sudden appearance of the cliff in front of him helped immensely) and turned. There was no one to be seen. Drawing his sword he shouted at the shadows, "Show yourself, villain!"

"As you wish." A dark knight stepped out of the shadows, blackened sword and mail gleaming in the moonlight, and attacked.

Wain halted his headlong rush at the edge of the cliff too. Between suddenly having nowhere to run to and nothing behind him to run from he felt that over all it was time to stop. He was considering his options when he realized a terrible truth. He, a warrior of the Mountain Top clan, had fled from the enemy and left a friend to be slain. Anger flowed through him and he drew his blade, the ringing sound it made echoing the singing in his blood. Hearing the clash of swords nearby Wain strode forth with grim resolve.

Sir James was hard pressed, sword play had never been his strong point. He had always been better at leading Vespers. At the beginning of the fight he had scored a few hits against the dark knight and his sword was gleaming wetly, but now he could barely defend himself. The Vampire cackled evilly as it increased the ferocity of its attack. Knocking James' sword from his hand, the evil warrior prepared to plunge his blade into the paladin's heart. James, in a burst of inspiration, fell to his knees and prayed for light. A holy white flame appeared above his head and lit the cliff's edge. The vampire turned his head with a cry, momentarily blinded. Wain rushed out of the night and swung his sword. With his target clearly illuminated it was simple to separate the vampire's head from its body. As the headless corpse fell to the ground they could hear a rushing sound and see green bale-fire flickering about its severed neck.

"Well, that was close," said James trying to appear nonchalant as he wiped down his blade.

"You shouldn't have run away," said Wain, cleaning his sword on the vampire's cloak.

"I was practicing strategic withdrawals," said James coldly. "Next time we need to stick together."

They were walking back to camp as they talked and suddenly Wain said, "Look! There's someone roasting a sausage over our fire!"

"Be careful."

"I'll just pin him to the tree." Wain strung his bow and knocked an arrow.

"No! He might be from the Order of the Sea."

"All right. If you don't want me to shoot him." Wain grumbled, put the bow down, and strode into the camp. He grabbed the stranger, slammed him against the tree, and pinned him to it with his arm. In his other hand he caught the sausage.

"What are you doing here?" he growled.

"I am a knight of the Order of the Sea," stuttered the man.

"Oh, really?" Wain stared at the man.

"Just let him down, Wain," James said. "I sense no danger in him."

"Oh ok." Wain let the man go and took a bite of the sausage. "Sorry about that."

"Oh, no trouble, I'm sure." The man looked nervously at the barbarian.

"Sit down," James invited. "What can you tell us about the tower guard?"

"The local garrison is led by a vampire, it consists of ten soldiers. Under the tower is a passage to the center island where the main fortress is."

"How fares your order?"

"We have ten trained knights, ready to do or die to free the islands."

"Are you their leader?"

"No. Our leader is Alain Shiningblade."

"Why is he called Shiningblade?" Wain licked the sausage grease from his fingers.

"It sounds better than Shiningknife," said the man. "You see, all we have are our daggers, bucklers, and wooden training swords."

"Once we deal with the tower garrison tomorrow then you will all be properly armed," assured Wain.

"We will be glad to follow you, lord paladin. Alain instructed me to tell you that he hopes you will use us wisely. He does not believe that we have the weaponry or the skill to match against the soldiers, without heavy casualties. Especially the vampire."

"We have slain the vampire already," James said.

"Truly? You seem not injured."

"A dorky looking fellow in a black cloak, with blackened weaponry. Right?" Wain asked.

"I wouldn't call them dorky..." Said the man hesitantly.

"Yeah well, he's dead," Wain glared.

James broke in. "Tomorrow we will deal with the garrison. Go tell Alain that we will meet him at noon in the village and assault the tower."

"Yes, milord paladin." The man rose and left.

Both James and Wain fell asleep almost immediately. It had been a long two days for they had not slept in the boat. Fortunately for them the vampire had ordered his soldiers to stay in the tower until his return. They were happy enough to comply. Even though they were hardened mercenaries, the vampires committed tortures that turned their stomachs.

James woke the next day slightly before noon and rolled over stiffly. This was what he hated most about these adventures. He always forgot to take off his armor before sleeping and the ground was uncomfortable to begin with. He stretched, straining his muscles almost to the point of cramping. Then he woke Wain and they walked down to the village to

Three Times Lucky ❀

meet the Order of the Sea. Their leader, Alain Shiningblade, stepped out to meet them.

"Greetings, O Holy Warriors. We are ready to follow your lead. I have but one question."

"What is that?" asked James. Wain was still rubbing the sleep from his eyes.

"How are we to storm the tower? It has a heavy door that is the only entrance and is barred from the inside. It will take over an hour to cut through it and we have no ram."

"My friend here," James indicated Wain, who yawned, "will show how with faith in the Lord and a little cunning one can overcome the greatest of obstacles. Go ahead Wain."

"Open the door? All right. One open door coming right up."

Wain trotted up to the door and, ducking his shoulder, slammed into it. The knights stared in disbelief as the stocky barbarian bounced off the solid oak planks. Wain crashed into the door again and again was thrown back. As he prepared for his third rush however, the door swung open and a guard glared out.

"Stop this infernal..." A surprised look crossed his face. "Who are you?"

Wain punched him in the nose and dove through the open doorway, sword flashing. The knights cheered and James led them charging in after Wain. They burst into the bottom floor, but all that remained was corpses. The sound of steel clashing together could be heard above.

❧ Byron Gordon

"Five here and five with me," yelled James, "Come on men..."

As he ran up the stairs James realized that none of the knights were following him. They were all retching at the sight of the freshly dead. James sighed and turned to continue up the stairs. He was halted by a blood soaked barbarian standing at the top.

"The building is clear, James."

"Even the sentry?" A sodden thump outside confirmed that the sentry had been taken care of.

"The main passage is through the trapdoor here, Sir James," Alain looked pale but otherwise recovered.

"Arm yourselves and onward." James led the charge down into the passage. "Try to stay closer this time Wain."

"You guys got left behind, not me." Wain shouted back at him.

The passage soon split and James sent the young knights off to liberate the other island, while he and Wain continued on to the main stronghold. The tunnel ended at a large stone gate, locked tight. On the steps leading up to the gate sat a weary looking old man. At least, that is what Wain saw.

James saw a powerfully built man, clad in dark armor sitting on the step. A mace rested in his lap and his eyes were as black and hateful as a beetles.

"Why are you here?" groaned the old man.

"To slay the vampires." Stated Wain with pride.

"I am their gatekeeper." Moaned the old man. "If you promise to set me free I will open the gate for you."

Three Times Lucky ❧

"I swear on the sword of my fathers that you will be set free." Said Wain. James, for some peculiar reason known only to himself said nothing about the delusion that Wain was under.

The old man unlocked the gate and held it open. Wain and James started to pass through and as soon as their backs were to him the dark knight dropped the delusion and swung his mace at the paladin's head. James, who had been expecting just such an attack, dodged and the mace missed.

Wain whirled, outraged at having been tricked, a deadly barbaric rage filling him. But James saw more dark knights rushing down the corridor to out flank them and shouted, "Watch my back Wain!"

Wain whirled again, his sword singing through the air, and he rushed the group of dark knights, cutting one down and smashing another over the head. His sword shattered and the knights, after their instinctive recoil from his sudden charge, began to close in. With a mighty leap Wain pushed past them and tore an enormous stone sword from where it was mounted on the wall.

Terrified by the display of strength the vampires broke and fled back from whence they had come. Wain chased after them, right on their heels. He crushed the slowest knight with the stone sword before they rounded the corridor, swatting him like a fly.

The vampires fled, seeking a place where they could be safe and regroup. Wain followed, an unstoppable force of nature, hacking and hewing

❧ Byron Gordon

them from behind. The last knight made it to a door and slammed it shut. Panting he leaned into the door and held it closed. He never expected that stone sword to burst through and cleave the door in half, crushing him in the process.

Wain strode into the room, the red light fading from his eyes as no more enemies stood before him. A quick glance around the room convinced him that the only object of interest was the treasure chest. It gleamed with light from within and was heavily locked. Wain hefted the stone sword and stepped closer.

Meanwhile Sir James was fighting with the leader of the vampires. He was slowly but surely getting better at the whole sword fighting part of his life. He was giving as good as he got but couldn't parry the dark knight's mace. As he ducked and counter attacked James thought of the fight from the night before. He muttered a prayer for light under his breath as he ducked another swing. The white, holy flame appeared above his head, its rays filling him with strength and his enemy with fear. With a final mighty stroke Sir James Flickerflame smote the dark knight right sorely and drove him to the ground, breaking his opponent's back.

"Nice shot." James whirled to see who spoke.

"Easy there. It's me." Wain hefted his treasures. "Look at what I found."

"The sword and shield!" gasped James.

"Yup. And since I broke my sword and I need another one..."

"No! We must give the artifacts to the Bishop. They are sorely needed on the front."

"How do we get back?"

"Let's go get those young knights and have them sail us back in the warship that is conveniently stored in a hidden harbor over there."

"How did I guess we would end up on another boat," sighed Wain.

"Pater et Filius et Spiritus Sanctus," chanted Wain. Although he would never admit it to James he liked Vespers. The snack hour afterward was great, hard to beat free food. He also enjoyed the chants, even if they were hard to learn.

The Fertile Plain

From Dref Cefel, Bishop of Chastity
Member of the Holy Council
Greetings, Most Honored Paladin,

After your skillful recovery of the Sword of Light and the Holy Shield from the Vampiric Archipelago The Holy Council has discussed what your next task should be, and have decided, through the Grace of God, that you should, with the same courage and fortitude you have displayed in all of your endeavors, journey to the continent, that den of evil and iniquity, and make your way, with care and discretion, to the land that is known as the Fertile Plain. Once there you shall, with bravery and initiative, reclaim the lands, for they produce much food, so that we might feed our armies in the field. Sadly I am very busy and cannot answer any questions you might have, so you should direct your inquiries, if you should have

ცვ Byron Gordon

any, to a man who you will find, if you need to look, at the Broken Limb, a most rough but goodhearted place. His name is Ralph Betternot. Now go with my blessing and win another great victory for the Council,

Dref Cefel
Bishop of Chastity
M. H. C.

"Well. What's it say?" Wain looked expectantly at Sir James.

"Here." James tossed the parchment to his companion.

Wain threw it right back. "Come on, just tell me what it says."

"Just read it," grumbled James.

"Because reading is not a skill worthy of a warrior of the mountain and," Wain looked embarrassed, "I can't read. Ok."

"Oh." James shook his head. He kept forgetting how ignorant his barbarian friend was. "Ok."

He had to read the message to Wain twice before the barbarian broke into a wide smile and said, "So we're going to a bar. Huzzah."

"Wain, we are at a bar," James reminded him.

"No, this is an inn," Wain explained patiently. "There are rooms for travelers to stay in. A bar has no rooms, just booze." He shook his head. He kept forgetting how ignorant his paladin friend was.

"Ok, fine. Let us go to this bar and talk to Betternot. Betternot what, I wonder?"

Three Times Lucky ⁊

"Betternot want us to buy him drinks, that's what," said Wain.

"Well." James rose from the remains of their breakfast. "Maybe you had betternot come."

"Oh no," replied Wain quickly. "You won't know how to hang out in a bar. I'd better go along and make sure that you don't get in trouble."

"Oh, I see." James strode through the door and down the street. "I can take care of myself, thank you very much."

"James," called Wain, pointing in the opposite direction. "It's this way."

"How do you know that?"

"I just asked the barmaid."

"Oh." James paused. "Well I was going to walk around the block first, that breakfast seemed rather heavy and I must keep in shape. Toodle-oo!" He sauntered back off the wrong way. Wain followed at a discreet distance to make sure that he kept out of trouble. By the time they arrived at the Broken Limb Wain keenly felt the need for a beer. He started to feel better the minute they walked into the rough, but goodhearted establishment.

It certainly was a rough place. Wain strode through several fist fights on his way to the bar, brushing the local toughs aside like flies, his powerful physique discouraging retaliation. He discovered shortly after sitting at a corner table with James and Betternot that the beer was excellent and he leaned back while James questioned Betternot.

"I am to go the Fertile Plain and reestablish communications with them. Anything you can tell me about the place?"

"Well." Betternot sipped his beer. "The entire area is squished between two rivers. There used to be bridges in and out but I haven't been there for a while. It's an odd place. The Church doesn't like it known but there are actually several tribes of orcs out there that manage to get along with the humans well enough. It used to be quite a rich area, due to the amount of grain they put out. Their local badge is a stalk of wheat on a green field. Another thing that is not common knowledge is that the Church already sent out a party to do this. There were four or five experienced crusaders who went out while you were working over that archipelago. We haven't heard from them since before they crossed the river. That is really all I know, thanks for the beer." Betternot rose from his chair and seemed to disappear before James' eyes into the crowded bar room.

"What do we do?" asked Wain.

"Five experienced crusaders died out there," James spoke miserably. "What hope do we have?"

"So we stay here and drink some more beer?" suggested Wain, hopefully.

"Nay." James restored some of the confidence that paladins are famous for to his voice. "My honor shalt ne'r be sated till this task is accomplished. With bravery and fortitude we shall carry on." He got up and headed for the door with a stony face.

Three Times Lucky ౭

"Why are you talking all funny?" inquired Wain as he followed.

"It was supposed to sound inspiring," said James.

Wain had no response to this. Instead he chewed on a piece of meat that he stole from a street vendor's cart.

"You just ate breakfast!" protested James. Suddenly he clapped his hands to his head. "Oh no! I have been drinking, and before midday! What will the Holy Council say?!"

"Relax, they'll just say," Wain swallowed, "There goes a seasoned warrior. Know how they know. You get your drinks when you can and don't expect to get back for more." He grinned like this was a cheerful piece of news.

"We are going to die," James said in a distant and miserable voice (he seemed to be developing quite a talent for it). "And my only assistance is a crazed barbarian."

"Yes," responded Wain heartily, slapping James on the back. "Crazed by hunger and thirst for adventure and…"

Speaking back and forth with all the fervor and warmth of old friends they continued their way to the quays where they found a boat waiting to take them to the mainland, that den of evil and iniquity!

✦

A week later a very green barbarian and a rather pale paladin stepped off the vessel and into the bustling business town of Sisal. While Wain chased down a street urchin (of the unprickily variety) who had picked James' pocket, James found a hostler and swiftly became engaged in a full blown battle to prevent being hustled.

"I do not want the dun… No not the battle stallion either… I do not care if he carried Deuteromo of the Shining Sword into his last battle, that just means that the poor fool was killed while this horse was… No, all I want is a pair of riding ponies and a pack mule… Yes with shoes and tack… No, no tack with silver and gold woven into the bridles… No! No diamonds, just plain steel and leather will be… If you even dare to offer me that black studded leather harness then I will burn your stable to the ground and give it to the punks that like that kind of junk! Now just get me what I WANT!!!!"

"O, Ah sa'h, sah." The hustling hostler stepped back and blinked. "Ah must sa'h Ah al'a'hs thought tha' you paladins ware gentlemeeen."

"Just get me my darn stuff!" Hollered James, beyond control for once in his life.

"O, right choo are sah. Ah'll jest go get it then, shall Ah?" The hostler hurried to the back of the barn and returned shortly with the desired goods. By the time he got back James had regained control and was stiffly readjusting his surcoat. Wain arrived at the same time, looking rather scratched and red in the face but with a triumphant battle light shining from his eyes.

"Sah, if Ah might recommend…"

"Is this all we want?" Wain asked James.

Three Times Lucky

"Yes." James sulked.

"Then that'll do, and don't you even think of trying to sell us something we don't want. Do you know what I did to the last man who tried that with me?"

The hostler shook his head.

"I hunted him down and chewed on his face! Have you ever had your face chewed on by a barbarian? Well its no joy ride!"

The hostler wiped his brow with a stained cloth as the pair walked away. He thanked his lucky stars that he came through that without losing anything. He must have barely glimpsed the troubled and violent soul that lurked beneath the tranquil expression on the paladins face. Especially if the man could stand to keep company with face chewing barbarians!

After a week of riding and camping in the open, Sir James and Wain arrived upon the banks of Western Edge, one of the two great rivers that secluded the Fertile Plain from the rest of the continent. They had been following a rough road that was marred by deep ruts. It looked as if the road had been the main shipping route for the grain that the Fertile Plain produced in great abundance. But all the wagon tracks were old, with no newer ones to cover them.

The road led them to the foot of what had once been a mighty bridge. Crumbled stone pillars stretched across the span of the river and hinted at the height the bridge had once risen too. It looked as though the stone from the bridge had been cast into the water forming a ford. Every sense in James' body told him that danger lurked amongst the shadows cast by the remains of the bridge.

"Let us go see if there is another ford, farther up the river," he told Wain.

"What's wrong with this one?" qestioned Wain. "The water is slow, it is not deep, and even if it flash floods the pillars will keep us from being swept away."

"I don't like it. It is too quiet," said James, guiding his shaggy pony, whom he had affectionately named Doubting Thomas, away and up stream.

"Ok, ok," Wain shouted as he followed. "We'll try to find another ford. But I don't see why you're being such a wuss."

"I am being smart," retorted James.

They came upon another ford at midday. Once again there had been a bridge crossing the river but it too had been demolished, even more efficiently than the one before. The only sign that there had been a bridge was the stone that formed the bed of the ford. Once again James felt the danger that lurked around the ford. He turned to go further upstream.

"What, you don't like this one either?"

"There is danger here," stated James in a calm tone.

"You're right, we could drown, or once we get across we could be ambushed by whatever destroyed the bridge or a bolt of lightning could just randomly crash down from the sky and electrocute us both,"

Three Times Lucky

ranted Wain. "You silly paladins are always afraid, sensing danger in everything, when there is always danger. You could suddenly faint and fall off your horse and break your neck. How do you know that is not the danger you sense?"

"Well." James paused. "I don't like these banks, the ponies couldn't climb them quickly if they had to."

"Come on, lets just get across. At the moment I am ready for some danger. I've been itching for action since this morning."

"We are going to die," stated James in his miserably distant voice as he guided his pony down the slippery bank.

Wain joined him at the bottom of the bank and they started across the ford. James felt a sudden, horrifying foreboding and then the water to their right side exploded as a giant troll sprang up from where it had been crouched. The ponies leapt roughly ten feet into the air, casting their passengers into the water, and were back up the bank so fast that James could have sworn that they had teleported.

Wain leapt to his feet, his long sword already in his hands. James picked himself up slightly slower and drew his own sword. He was about to rush the troll but the troll rushed first, smacking Wain with one huge paw and slamming him into the muddy bank. James swiftly assaulted the trolls right flank, cutting a long slash down the monsters leathery green back.

With a roar that made the waters tremble the troll whipped around and swatted James like a large mosquito. The brave paladin was flung against the far bank and he swore that he could hear his ribs cracking. His vision was dim and he could barely make out that the troll was coming after him. He tried to get up but his arms would not move. He muttered a prayer of healing and felt his ribs restore themselves to their proper location, desperately trying to ready himself for the next attack.

With a resounding bellow that caused the river water to back up upon itself, leaving the river-bed dry for a brief instant, Wain flung himself against the trolls exposed back. He hewed with the strength of a dozen men and his movements were faster than the wild cats that inhabited the mountains of his home.

The troll roared again in anger and turned, smashing a giant fist into the short barbarians body. James could hear the bones popping and the armor crushing but Wain seemed not to notice. A red light shone in his eyes and with a mighty swing he lopped off the trolls arm. With a roar of pain the monster clutched at his severed shoulder, then backhanded Wain with a blow that would have shattered a city gate. The barbarian took the strike and shrugged it off as if saying, is that the best you can do?

Then, almost faster than James' eye could follow Wain planted his foot against the troll's humongous thigh and jumped up to the monster's eye level. Executing a complete midair spin, Wain severed the beast's ugly head from its scaly shoulders. He dropped lightly to the ground, drenched in green troll blood. Then, adroitly dodging the troll's falling body, which

Three Times Lucky

fell with a ground shuddering thud, he started to rush at James!

"Now Wain," James shouted, trying to remain calm. "This is James. I am your friend. Calm down. Relax."

Wain halted his charge a few scant feet from Sir James, sword raised to strike, as the red light slowly faded from his eyes. James began to say another prayer of healing, only this time for Wain.

"James, I." Wain toppled like a pole axed ox, his terrible injuries finally overcoming him. He woke later that night lying next to a fire, his sword still tightly gripped in his hand. James had removed the scabbard from his belt and sheathed the sword.

"What happened?" Wain tried to raise his head but it pounded too much and he lay back down.

"Never seen anything like it," replied James in a troubled voice. "It was like you were possessed. You should have been crushed three times but you just seemed to soak up the blows. It was like you went berserk or something."

"Oh." Wain could still feel the enchanting cry for battle singing in his veins. "I think that is maybe exactly what I did."

"I have heard," said James. "That some of your cousins who serve in the Continental Army are like that. The commanders use them as one shot missiles, sending them against the enemy before the proper charge to loosen up the enemy line. I have never heard of them coming back after being sent forth."

"That is because they are weaklings who serve fools." Wain could feel strength flowing back into his limbs and the pounding in his head eased. "Ok, I killed the troll and now we are here. What is our next move?"

"I think there is a town near here. Tomorrow we can go check it out, see what's going on in this place."

"Sounds like fun," Wain said. "Do we have any food? I'm starving!"

"Here." James handed him some jerked fish and a loaf of bread. "This is all we have."

"Mmmff." Wain tore through the food. "Makes a good incentive to find the town I guess." He swallowed the last of the food and lay back down. "Goodnight." He was soon snoring.

James slept lightly, partly due to Wain's snoring, partly so that his ability to feel danger before it arrived would awake him in case there was need.

The next morning dawned bright and clear, with birds twittering and swooping for worms. Wain was already awake, checking over his ponies tack and harness. James rubbed a mixture of sleep, grime, and dew from his eyes as he sat up.

"Ready to go?" asked Wain. "There's the village over that way. You can see the smoke from their morning fires. Lets hurry and get there, I'm starving."

"A paladins life is one of self-deprivation," James said coldly, for he had gone without dinner and did not wish to think about food. "We must focus beyond the desires of our flesh and on the greater goal."

Three Times Lucky ∞

"Good." Wain mounted his pony. "That means you won't eat when we get food. More for me! Hyaa!"

He rode off into the rising sun.

"That is not quite what I meant," muttered James, hurrying to mount up and ride after his friend, but he was hampered by the pack mule, and did not catch up until Wain paused a mile outside of the village.

"Well, at last you stopped long enough for me to catch up." James paused, seeing a hint of the red battle light in Wain's eyes. "What is it now?"

"James," said Wain through gritted teeth. "There are orcs in that village. Orcs in charge of humans. This is not right. I must kill!"

"Calmly Wain," cautioned James. "We don't know if they are the friendly orcs that Betternot told us about or not."

"They'd better not be." Wain was holding his sword's hilt, though he did not draw, "I just saw one of them beating an old woman."

"What!" James' sense of justice was stirred and he lost his head. Without another thought he gave the order. "Charge Wain, we will sweep them from the face of the earth!"

"Hyaa!" Wain charged forward, with James bringing up the rear again.

Their initial rush took the orc garrison by surprise. James cut down two hapless soldiers and then looked around. He was just in time to see Wain performing a complicated move that involved disemboweling the orc behind him, cutting the legs off the orc to his right, kicking the orc on the left in the teeth, and

↪ Byron Gordon

beheading the orc in front of him. All of this was accomplished in less time than it takes to tell, the barbarian's body moving like a blazing whip. This move terrified all of the villagers except for one. That particular villager found it fascinating and, after years of practice, developed a style of dancing based upon it. It was named break dancing for the effect of Wain's boot smashing through the orcs skull.

The remaining orc soldier gave a cry of terror and fled into the fields beyond. Wain was upon him like a hound dog upon a ham bone. James followed as swiftly as possible to prevent Wain from hurting any of the villagers. He arrived on the scene just in time to miss how the orc had been split into six pieces by three sword strokes that followed so fast upon one another that they seemed to be one.

"Wain!" shouted James. "Relax! You have killed all the enemy!"

With a roar Wain charged at James. Doubting his safety James started to back up, very quickly, while trying to calm down his friend. It is very difficult to walk backwards quickly on uneven ground and James tripped, dropping to the ground with a thud. He shook his head and started crawling backwards while still trying to calm his friend. Wain was standing over him with sword raised when the red light finally faded from his eyes.

"James." Wain looked down at him. "Why are you crawling around on the ground like a worm?" He offered his hand to pull up his friend.

Three Times Lucky

"You need to learn to control your anger," snapped James.

"I know." Wain scuffed his feet against the ground. "I'll try harder next time."

"See that you do. Now let's go talk to the villagers before you go crazy and kill them all."

"Ok," Wain mumbled. "I saved them from the orcs though."

"Excuse me." James ignored Wain and called to the village elder. "Excuse me, I am Sir James Flickerflame, Humble Paladin of the Holy Isle and I was wondering…"

"Where your friends are?" the elder interrupted. "Of course, well, doncha know, it was just the other day that they came through, four of them, doncha know, all with a lot of armor and impressive weaponry and stuff, doncha know, just like any crusader who has been campaigning would have been, and they wanted to know what was going on around here, doncha know, so I told them about Baldpate and that spooky tower he lives near, I mean, anything to oblige, doncha know, and then they thanked me very much, don…"

"If you say doncha know one more time," said Wain through gritted teeth. "Then I will reduce you to a red wet rag!"

"Well, I say, rather you didn't do that old chap," stuttered the elder. "Anyhow, like I was saying, they thanked me and then said that they'd see what they could do about freeing us, don…" He stopped suddenly, as Wain was beginning to sound like a boiling tea kettle.

"Easy Wain." James patted his shoulder. "You must forgive him, his mother was a bit of an ogre."

"I see," the elder gasped. "Well, I say, rather a touchy sort of chap, but anyhow, old fellow, they left and we haven't seen them since, although I heard one of them say that they should set up a camp somewhere they couldn't be found easily."

"Like a forest?" whistled Wain.

"Well, yes, rather like a forest."

"Where is the nearest forest?" asked James.

"To the south." The elder pointed.

"Let us go Wain. I want to know what happened to those guys."

"Ok, let's go." Wain leaped up onto his horse and started to ride again, only to rein the poor beast in suddenly.

"What's the matter now?" asked James, eager to be away.

"I just remembered," said Wain. "We didn't get any food."

"Here, we made up a package of food for you just in case," said the elder. "It's already on your pack horse. It was the least we could do, Godspeed."

The two heroes and three horse cantered away south towards the forest, reaching the shady eaves by nightfall. They dismounted and led their noble steeds into the forest a few hundred feet where they decided to camp for the night.

Three Times Lucky ☙

The next morning James led them deeper into the forest, feeling drawn by a strange force. They soon arrived upon a lean-to built up against a pair of large trees. A fire ring filled with ashes was laid out in front of the structure. The ashes were still relatively fresh.

"Hmm." Wain studied the ash with a keen eye. "Not two days old I should say, came from a two hundred year old oak branch, if I'm not mistaken."

"How can you tell that?" demanded James.

Wain waved his hand in the air. "Elementary my dear James!"

"Oh shut up!" said James.

"What are we looking for here?" asked Wain, his Holmes-like manner abandoned as suddenly as it had appeared.

"A clue, message, something like that."

"How about this dead guy in the lean-to?"

"Oh my, how did he get there?"

"Looks like he crawled. See the tracks lead down to that little creek. I'd say that he was injured and was expecting an attack. He is still wearing his armor."

"Check him over, see if he has left any messages."

"Ooh, this is some nice armor."

"No Wain, we are not stealing his gear," James snapped.

"But he don't need it."

"That is not the point."

"Fine." Wain never argued points with James. He always lost. "But look at this nice sword." Wain handed the sword back to James.

"Yes, excellent steel, I'd say." James drew the blade and almost dropped it as it burst into white flame. "Well, I say!"

"What?" Wain looked up from his study of the corpse.

"What do you mean?"

"What do you say?"

"What?"

"Before."

"When?" James asked.

"Just now."

"What are you talking about?"

"No, what are you talking about? That's what I'm talking about," said Wain.

"What?" James threw his hands up in exasperation.

"You already said that. Besides I said it first."

"What?"

"Exactly," Wain snapped.

"Exactly what?"

"James, just forget about it. Forget I ever said it." Wain started searching the lean-to.

James shook his head and practiced sheathing and drawing the sword to see the flames burst forth. It was truly a crusaders weapon, the weapon of a master swordsman. Not to mention it was really cool. James began to belt it on his sword belt when Wain pitched out of the lean-to with a loud shriek. James dropped the sword and Wain yelled again, having landed on the fire ring and all of the pointy rocks in it. He rolled

Three Times Lucky

off the rocks to the base of a nearby tree, groaning loudly.

"What…"

"Don't start that again!" Wain yelled.

"I was just going to say 'What…'"

"No, don't say it."

"But what…"

"Zip it!"

"Fine! Who threw you out of the lean-to?"

"No one."

"Then what…"

"STOP!" Bellowed Wain, with a terrible look on his face.

A poor squirrel, frightened stiff, fell out of a tree and onto its head. With a crunch. Wain suddenly guffawed, the terrible look faded and his normal, constipated look returned. Then he remembered what had happened and looked scared.

"There was a rune in there and I didn't want to be contaminated."

"Well, you should have said so. What…"

"Don't say it, just look at the rune."

"Ok, ok, ok." James leaned into the lean-to apprehensively and saw the rune carved upon one of the posts. "Hello there, you little devil you."

"Hello," replied the rune in a deep voice.

"Oh my…" James cracked his head on the upper beam and fell onto his rear. "Ow."

"We were ambushed in the maze at the bottom of the tower. There were many skeletons and a dark spirit of tremendous power."

"Wain do you hear something?"

"Yeah I hear you talking in a normal voice and then a deep voice trying to scare me and guess what, it won't work… Aah, the rune is talking, we are going to go to the bad place of fire and flame!" Wain started hopping up and down like a rather comical monkey.

"Be very careful when you assault the tower and… my strength is almost gone. I must end the blessing. Good luck and farewell." The rune faded leaving only a scorched mark on the post.

"It is a warning," mused James. "Left by this crusader. How could a holy warrior use an unholy skill like runic enchantments?"

"Stupid warning. Be careful," Wain snorted, apparently recovered from his attack of the willies. "What else is new?"

"We shall have to be careful when we go there," James continued musing, as he buckled the flaming sword to his belt. "And we should bury the remains of this valiant warrior."

"Ok, I'll start digging and then…" Wain trailed off. "Why do you get his sword but I don't get his armor?"

"That is not the point."

"Oh. Ok."

They buried the body of the crusader in the soft loam of the forest and then rested until night fell.

"Let us go, we can assault the tower under the cover of darkness. They will never expect that."

Three Times Lucky ☙

"Why are we attacking skeletons and a dark spirit of tremendous power at night," muttered Wain as he led his horse after James. "They're scary enough during the day."

"Don't worry Wain, we will be fine," James shouted back to him.

"How does he do that?" Wain muttered as the darkness of the night swallowed them.

Once clear of the forest they mounted their horses and rode off into the moon rise, towards the tower of doom.

As they rode closer to the tower they began to feel more and more like maybe the should leave and come back tomorrow. Or next week. Or next month. Or next year.

"Uh, James," said Wain.

"Don't even suggest it," James snapped. "The tower is casting a spell upon us as a means of defense."

"Ugh," agreed Wain, reduced to one syllable words by his unease.

They left their horses there, and walked the last mile in to the tower. It was very tall and made of black basalt. The stones seemed to exude a nauseating aura.

"It me sick." Wain was still only using single syllables.

"Do not go berserk in here, ok?" James cautioned him. "This mission calls for stealth."

"Wain no get mad," Wain nodded. "Wain got it."

"Ok. We will sneak in through this little side door."

"It only door."

"Ok. We will sneak through this little main door," James repeated, "And surprise them."

"Ok, Wain like."

James opened the door cautiously and barely refrained from cursing as it creaked. The interior of the tower was pitch black and so James said a quick prayer for light. With the little flame of light hovering over his head they proceeded carefully down the interior passage only to come to a split. It was a maze.

"Darn."

"Wain no cuss, why James?"

"Here take my blessed cloak." James draped the cloak over Wain, "It will make you invisible to the undead. Use your bow and shoot anything that comes near."

"Ok," Wain said. Wain draped the cloak about his shoulders and strung his bow. The intrepid pair crept deeper into the maze.

"Wain!"

"What?"

"I see something!"

"I'll shoot it, hang on!"

"Yeourgh!!!!"

"I think that is a dead skeleton now!" Wain chuckled, the familiarity of combat relieving his tension.

"Good shot."

They continued throughout the maze, easily destroying the skeletons that they encountered until, by a incredible amount of luck they reached a set of

Three Times Lucky ಏ

stairs. Not knowing how else to proceed, they climbed up the winding steps to a room at the very top of the tower. In the corner of the room a dark shadow flinched upon the sight of James' holy light. Then it spoke in a strange tongue, the holy light went out, and utter darkness enveloped them.

"Aah!" Wain fled back down the stairs.

"Thanks Wain," shouted James as he drew his sword. White flame burst forth from the blade and illuminated the room.

James thought he heard the evil spirit grumble: "Oh not this guy again."

The paladin rushed to the attack, swinging his sword with deadly skill and fervor. Although he struck twice the spirit merely grunted and punched him, a strong blow right in the face. James fell back, lip bleeding, and shook his head, trying to clear it of the stars that had suddenly appeared.

The spirit was coming in for the finish when an arrow appeared out of nowhere and burst into flame as it struck the shadow. The spirit howled and looked around for his attacker. James could see Wain crouched near the head of the stairs, hidden from the spirit by the cloak. Another arrow struck the spirit and with a snarl it started to hurl black lances in the general direction of the stairs. They all struck over Wain's head but his face looked a little pale.

James rallied his strength and attacked the spirit once again, his fiery sword leaving a trail of light as he swung it through the air. This time he dodged the spirit's punch and cut away again. Then the spirit caught him off guard with four simultaneous punches. James ducked two but was flung against the wall by the force of the two blows that struck home.

Wain loosed another arrow and struck the spirit square on the back. With a stone grinding shriek that shook the tower to its core the spirit burst into flames and disappeared. Wain came over to James and helped him to his feet. While James muttered a healing prayer, Wain found a ladder to the roof of the tower and they climbed up to rest in the fresh air for the rest of the night.

In the morning they were woken by a loud voice screaming in a strange language. They peered over the edge and saw a large bald ogre standing over roughly twenty orcs. The ogre was shouting at them and the orcs were doing pushups.

"He-he. Watch this," Wain chuckled and, before James could stop him, shot an arrow at the ogre.

The ogre yelled with surprise as the wooden shaft stuck in his butt and looked up at the top of the tower.

"You sissy little man," shouted the ogre to Wain, amongst other insults. "Come down and fight like an ogre!"

"Ignore him Wain," James said. "He's just trying... WAIN!"

The red light of battle once again flooding his eyes, Wain leapt from the roof of the tower down to the ogre and the orcs. He drew his sword as he fell, spinning like a deadly whirligig. James rushed down the ladder and then the stairs, trying to reach the

Three Times Lucky ಬ

ground before he was too late. He opened the door to the tower in the face of a startled orc and cut him down without a second glance. Then he saw the ogre hit Wain with a massive sword. A terrible gash was opened across Wain's chest but he seemed not to notice. James said his prayer of healing, and the wound closed, startling the ogre enough for Wain to lop off his arm. The ogres next blow cut off Wain's leg, and James said his prayer again and watched in amazement as the leg reattached itself. The ogre was just as amazed but swung again in fury. Wain actually blocked the blow, by accident, and the ogre's sword shattered, just before Wain cleaved him in half. The other nineteen orcs had already been slain and Wain looked around hungrily for other targets. He spied James and charged. James slammed the door shut and it shuddered under the impact of Wain's body slamming against it.

The rage did not fade from Wain's eyes until his sword had burst through the door. The blade quivered there for a moment, then was withdrawn and the blows seemed to have halted. James still waited a couple minutes before opening the door. Wain stood there, looking a little embarrassed.

"Sorry."

"It's ok. Good job." James patted his shoulder.

"Thanks."

"Let's go home."

"Ok."

✢

ᛓ Byron Gordon

"Well, I really must commend you for your bravery and skill. There were a couple times throughout your telling that I wasn't sure you would make it. It sounds like you have taught 'the barbarian' to follow you quite faithfully."

"Oh, it was nothing, Your Holiness," James said.

"No I really must congratulate you my boy, every time you go out it seems the quest is more and more difficult than the last one and yet you always prevail. You are a source of inspiration and pride for your entire sanctuary. You are becoming a bit of a celebrity in fact."

"It is nothing, Your Holiness," James repeated. "What is the next quest you have for me?"

"Nothing going on at the moment," said the Bishop. "Just rest and recover from your last ordeal."

"Of course." James backed out of the audience hall and met Wain outside the palace gates. Wain was sitting in the middle of a circle of little boys, who were listening spell bound as he told them how he had slain an evil troll on the continent. James noticed that all the boys held little Wain the Barbarian stick figures. None of them held any figures even remotely resembling a paladin.

"Come on Wain," James sighed. "Time to go."

"Aw!" cried the boys. "Can we come Wain?"

"No," said Wain. "You must all go home and wrestle and eat spinach to grow strong."

"Ok Wain!" The boys all ran off.

"You are becoming quite a role model," said James, just a little sourly.

Three Times Lucky ☙

"Oh, they don't mean any harm," chuckled Wain. "And they only hid their Sir James Flickerflame figures 'cause I told them to when you came out." Wain looked at a bar they were passing as he said this, hoping James did not spot the lie.

"You tricky guy you!" James grinned, his dark mood lifting.

"But they say I have cooler weapons," Wain laughed as he ducked into the next bar they passed.

James followed him in, just to keep his friend out of trouble, doncha know.

ABOUT THE AUTHOR

Byron Gordon grew up in the rural Eastern Shore of Maryland, USA. One of six children, he soon discovered his love of reading, ranging from the clever humor of P.G. Wodehouse to the epic fantasy of Tolkien to the fast paced science fiction of Timothy Zahn. Fed on this widely varied diet, his imagination blossomed and he began to write, desiring to create worlds and adventures of his own.

After realizing the bleak financial prospects of an aspiring writer trying to break into the fiction realm, Byron enlisted in the United States Coast Guard. He is still on active duty and currently plans search and rescue efforts on the east coast of the USA.

Despite the intense, and often hectic, schedule that military life entails, Byron has continued to write in his free time. In the spring of 2011, he started publishing his writings electronically and you may view his other work on his website at http://marieabmare.wordpress.com.

Made in the USA
Coppell, TX
04 July 2020

30077969R00042